The Réparateur
of Strasbourg

Ian R. MacLeod

The
Réparateur
of Strasbourg

The
Réparateur
of Strasbourg

Ian R MacLeod

Published in September 2013 by PS Publishing Ltd. by
arrangement with the author. All rights reserved by the
author. The right of Ian R MacLeod to be identified as
Author of this Work has been asserted by him in accordance
with the Copyright, Designs and Patents Act 1988.

First Edition

ISBN
978-1-848636-47-7
978-1-848636-48-4 (Signed Edition)

Design and Layout by Aaron Leis.
Printed and bound in England by T.J. International.
Set in Sabon and Colwell HPLHS.

PS Publishing Ltd
Grosvenor House / 1 New Road / Hornsea, HU18 1PG / England

editor@pspublishing.co.uk
www.pspublishing.co.uk

*T*HERE WAS ONCE A MAN NAMED EZEKIEL MOREL WHO WAS NO longer a man. Some claimed he was cursed forever to roam the earth, and that he fed upon human blood. Others, that he had been a great artist when properly alive. More often, though, it was said he was a creature out of a bad fairy tale and shouldn't exist at all. At least, not in these enlightened times.

The real Ezekiel Morel would never have claimed to be an artist, let alone a great one, although he was a painter of sorts. *Réparateur*, in the French which was then spoken in the city of Strasbourg where he'd once lived, was the correct term for what he did. He'd been apprenticed as an orphan to the trade of restoring the paintings and panels in churches, of which Strasbourg had, and still has, a great many.

"Ezekiel!"

He was a dreamer, and his old master Nesch would often slap him hard across the face for gazing out of the workshop window at the spires of that great, smoky city, or for watching the storks dance and clack their beaks as they rebuilt their rooftop nests. Still, Nesch knew talent when he saw it, and put the lad to work on the panel of the chapel of Our Lady of Sorrows in the church of Saint-Pierre-le-Jeune as the finishing piece of his apprenticeship. Not so much a restoration as a recreation, seeing as a leak from the roof had turned the sacred image to a blackened mess. But Ezekiel worked. Ezekiel laboured. The Madonna which emerged in fresh robes and a newly beguiling smile was greatly venerated. The storks in the landscape glimpsed behind her left shoulder as a symbol of the purity of motherhood were, it was agreed, a delightful touch, although few could recollect having seen them on the panel before.

1

Now Ezekiel could work on his own behalf, and with enough good favour amongst the lesser churches to establish a workshop. *E. Morel, Réparateur,* on a sign at street level that he had, of course, painted himself. He loved his new workshop, for all the many steps he had to climb to get to it. Loved its light and its fine views across the city. Loved the seasick slant of its wayward floor.

A grown man, now, and independent. Within a year, he had bought a full outfit of the kind of clothes that a prosperous craftsman might wear to gain admittance to a merchant's house, and ask for the hand of their youngest daughter in marriage. Within two, he had even found the courage to knock on the door of the particular merchant in question.

No one else but Ezekiel Morel thought Grete Matthinger beautiful. Not even her own father, who was dubious at first about his intentions. But Ezekiel cared enough for the rest of the world. They stood arm in arm one morning lined up with other artisan couples in the great, sacred space of the Cathedral of Our Lady, which was the tallest building in Christendom, and his heart blazed strong as the sun which made bonfires of the saints in the east windows. Great though Ezekiel's joy was, however, he still noticed the unravelling gilt of the bishop's seat, and the rust of its fixings, and how the tempura paint in the panelling depicting the deeds of Saint John beside the famous astronomical clock was showing tidemarks of damp.

They were married, and marriage was good. Awakening earlier than the birds on a summer's morning, and turning over, and finding once again—this was still a marvel to him—that he wasn't alone. Studying the sleep creases on Grete's face. The changes that came, as he breathed upon them, to the tips of her breasts. Then the church bells swung, and the city gates flung open, and Grete would yawn and smile at him, and stretch out her arms.

First came their twin daughters, Julie and Josette. Then a child which was stillborn and a great sorrow. Then they were blessed with a living son, whom they called Roland and cherished as the next in a thriving line of *réparateur* Morels. Especially when, even as a baby, Roland showed an aptitude for scrawling on a slate. A full family now, living in a building of beams scrolled with ropework carvings only a minute or so's walk from his workshop—at least, if you discounted that final climb up the stairs. Ezekiel forgave God for the loss of their first son because of the gift of Roland, and hoped that

God, in his wisdom, would forgive him. Knew enough about God, though, to understand that a man provided for his family unaided by any labours but his own.

The wood panelling on the cathedral's west wall was more mildewed than ever, although it doubtless looked fine to the untrained eye, and very little of the tempura which disguised the problem had yet flaked off. The first priest he spoke to was dismissive. The second even more so. It was only the third, just as Ezekiel was about to leave the place in fear of being put to the inquisition, who recognised the lad who'd worked on that Madonna in Saint-Pierre-le-Jeune, and was prepared to listen to what Ezekiel said.

Father Charbonneau was pinkly-plump, blonde-bearded and almost as young as Ezekiel. Unlike most priests, he had a practical bent. *Can use you here in this great house of the Lord, Ezekiel. Can probably use you for as long as you care to live. Glorious panels depicting the certainty of the resurrection that hid boring beetles. Statues of our Lord at the height of his suffering secured to the wall by little but prayer.* Father Charbonneau told Ezekiel that those in charge of the cathedral's fabric had perhaps been expecting Our Lord to establish his Kingdom on earth a little sooner than he had. That, and that the money which should have gone to seeing to these matters had often gone elsewhere.

Ezekiel prospered. The taxes the King levied on commoners were higher that ever, but he had regular work which allowed him to plan ahead, and he was a frugal man in everything but his ambition, which was to be the best *réparateur* in Strasbourg, which to his mind also meant all of France, and thus the entire world. He hired apprentices. He was a common sight inside cathedral. Directing things, or up ladders. He strode the markets and the docks, bargaining for fresh materials. The task was never done, and never could be, and that made him happy. Even his old master Nesch, had he still been living, would have been proud to see the man of means Ezekiel Morel had become.

Sometimes, though, the business of instructing others to do things he could better do himself, or trying to get the proper price for a block of Spanish resin from some thief of a merchant, and then returning home to find Julie and Josette dancing around Grete's feet, and little Roland howling, and the food not yet done, became wearing. It had always been his habit to perform the most delicate tasks up in his

3

high workshop. Stirring varnish, matching shades, sifting the best chalk for the final layer of gesso. When a particularly fine panel required his detailed attention, and sometimes simply because it was damaged beyond repair but too beautiful to see destroyed, he had it carried or winched up there and saw to it alone.

Ezekiel's workshop became a haven. On long summer evenings, or shivering in the coldest of winters with the gluepot fire in the corner burning and stinking but bringing little heat, he worked amid the rotting faces of saints and the broken wings of angels. One winter's dusk, he was there alone when he heard the distant groan of the door from the street and the swift creak of footsteps on the long flight of stairs. One of his apprentices had forgotten something? But these feet were too quick, too light. A thief? Ezekiel looked quickly about him. The last of the light had faded without him even noticing and he'd been working by little but a rising moon. He stood holding his pallet knife as the upper door creaked open, still telling himself it was probably nothing, nothing at all, and certainly nothing to be feared...

The figure was tallish for a woman, and she wore a cloak. In a pale flash of hands, she drew back her hood.

"Monsieur Morel."

A statement rather than a question. Ezekiel laid aside his pallet knife. He had seen this woman before, on a dark evening a month or so earlier as he teetered on a ladder against the south transept and the votive candles below glittered like the stars of an upturned sky. He remembered being overcome by a sense of being watched as he chipped away at some final loose flakes before finishing for the day. Looking down, he'd seen a cloaked figure, which he knew to be gazing up at him from the tilt of the hood which shadowed her face. There was so little of her to be seen, it struck him as extraordinary that he could recognise and recollect her as the same woman. But he could, and he did.

Now, in this rising moon, her hair fell gold across her shoulders in a manner which the more decent ladies of this city would have considered immoral, although Ezekiel thought he had never seen anything finer. If you discounted her face itself, that was. A perfect model, if he was looking for one, for the lost features of an angel, or some unknown saint. Eyes which were almond-shaped. Each slow blink a revelation, and the grey-irised heart of a gaze was so deep

4

and black that Ezekiel felt himself falling, just as he almost had up that ladder in the cathedral. There was something about the smile, as well, formed on those pink full-bowed lips, that was like no other smile he had ever seen. In fact, it was scarcely a smile at all, but some other expression that was neither sadness or joy. Her skin, in this moon-silvered light, was creamy-pale. But it had a duskiness as well. The craftsman in Ezekiel briefly wondered if it would be possible to match such a surface with any conceivable tint. If she hadn't been so real, if she hadn't been so feminine and simply *here*, he might even have wondered if she had come from some other realm.

Instead, though, he heard himself speaking of how this was a common workshop, and she had doubtless taken a wrong turn, and ascended these stairs under the impression that they led somewhere else, and that he would be forever indebted to her service if she permitted him the privilege of showing her back out. Not, of course, that he presumed—

"My name, Ezekiel," she said, cutting across his words, "is Ariadne. And I have a commission to ask of you."

Now, he supposed, his babble must have changed to talk of tim-escales and contracts. Of preparatory plans and bills of estimate for the works of restoration and repair of whatever chapel she required of him had been agreed.

"Repair? Restoration?" Her eyebrows her high and arched. "You are a painter, Ezekiel, are you not? I have seen your work in that fine panel of Our Lady at Saint-Pierre. I have never witnessed such storks—at least, those that did not clap their wings and take flight. Not to mention the face of Saint Cecelia as she raises it to heaven at the moment of her immolation in that panel in the south-western portal of this city's cathedral."

He couldn't deny that he was flattered. But he was also alarmed. Not that all the work she described wasn't his, at least in the sense that he had cleaned, refurbished and repaired it. But to use the word *painter* in the sense that she seemed to be doing was entirely wrong—in fact, downright dangerous—especially in a city where the guilds were rigorous in protecting their rights.

"Oh, enough of this foolish modesty!" Once again, she cut across his words, but this time with a flash of something close to wrath. "You sense that I want you to exceed the bounds of your normal duties, and you are right. But don't fool me, or yourself, Ezekiel, by

5

pretending that you are simply a craftsman, mutely reshaping that which is already there. There was no face at all to Saint Symphorian above the crossing tower in the cathedral before you put one there, and now the floor beneath him is strewn with the offerings of all this city who fear the venereal pox. Although to my mind your finest work is that detail of the rent in the world which lies beneath the feet of the Archangel Gabriel as he tramples Satan, and provides us with a glimpse of the terrors of Hell. Truly, if even in a miniature scale, you have the eye of Titian combined with the imagination of Bosch."

These were names Ezekiel knew little of, but he was flattered all the more. Curious, as well. He'd worked on that that concise vision of Hell in an odd kind of fever, without sketches or proper plan. Would have destroyed the thing had not Father Charbonneau seen it first and urged him not to.

"Oh, no," Ariadne said in response to the changed look on his face. "I have no desire for you to paint anything so horrible as that. At least, not yet. And you can turn down my request if you wish. I want you to accept freely—and if you do not, you will never see me again. But the one thing I do require of you is your absolute secrecy and discretion."

"What is it you wish me to do?"

"I want you to paint my portrait, Ezekiel. I want a small thing, mere head and shoulders. About..." she raised her hands. The shadows seemed to flutter about her like startled birds. "...this high by so wide. I understand that you are used to working on wood rather than on canvas. But a panel, the beginnings of a kind of triptych, is exactly what I require."

"Still, a society painter—"

"A society painter would strut and gossip and brag. All the more so if I asked for secrecy. And every one of those oafs that works in this city lacks in their entire bodies the skill that you have in your littlest finger. I will pay you well for your work, and you can say yes or you can say no. But if you accept, and if then you betray me and mention anything of me or this task to the world, woe betide you and your family."

Ezekiel nodded, although he was to wonder afterwards when exactly the moment had passed when he might have been able to say no. Then he bowed. "I am at your service."

"So we are agreed." Ariadne smiled, and moved toward him like beautiful smoke. Now, she was close by him, and her hand was on his shoulder. He had never felt anything so warm, nor so cold. "Do you think we could begin at about this time tomorrow evening, just you and I here in this same room?"

"I will be here."

"Good." She turned as if to leave. Then turned back to him as she pulled up her cloak. "Oh, and I do not want you to paint me as you see me now, Ezekiel. But as I will be in..." He sensed a small calculation within the shadows of her hood. "Twenty years."

"Should the good Lord preserve you," he heard someone with his own voice say as her footfalls departed into the gloom.

His name was Ezekiel Morel, and he was a *réparateur,* but he knew it was false modesty, and thus technically a sin, to pretend that he always merely repaired and refurbished the work of the blessed dead. Sometimes, on an area of cleaned old wood, or a piece of new surface he'd had to painstakingly fit where the timber was too rotted, he created that which had never been there. And sometimes, just as surely as he knew he loved his family and adored the colours of sunset, he knew that it was good.

Good, as well, to have this small project sideways from his regular work. Not least financially, with what you could buy in the markets costing more every day, and the girls always needing new shoes and Roland having a sensitivity, at least according to Grete, to wearing anything but silk. Not least because here was something, as he waited for the quick, light footfalls on the stairs leading to his workroom, which was his alone.

He wondered at first if he should complain at Ariadne's insistence on arriving when the day's light was gone. Although, as the evenings went by and he fell into his task—first making sketches and preparing precisely the right panel (after discarding many others) of good, well-seasoned walnut, then applying gesso and setting himself to the seemingly impossible task of finding the combination of shades with matched her skin, both so dark and yet so pale—he somehow felt he understood. Ariadne belonged to this time, and then to even deeper darkness into which she retreated at the end of each session. She was not a creature of the day.

He used the finest oils and pigments. Even when he was at other tasks, the shape of those lips, the deep gaze of those well-like eyes, was always close to the surface of his thoughts. It was, of course, a desecration to paint Ariadne as she had asked, but deep in those eyes, and in the turn of those lips that was neither happy nor sad, there was a sense of far greater years than those told by her other features. And she would still be beautiful, yes, twenty years from now. Beautiful for all the softening drag of lines and the droop of her shoulders which he was able to hint at as, layer upon layer, twilight upon twilight, he described the features of her perfect face.

He had her sit before the window which looked down and out on the square, where the King's soldiers would still sometimes parade. Captured her head and hair and shoulders in the rise of the moon. Thought for a while that, young or old, this light defined her as no other could. But then, as the painting grew before him, and the moon grew thin, and the window above the rooftops that she sat beside spilled with little more than a gleam of black, that it was the night itself that really framed and captured her, that darkness was where she and this portrait he could now sometimes barely see as he worked on it by the glimmer of the single candle, truly belonged.

Just head and hair and shoulders, although it was a secret of real painters that his old master Nesch had once shared with him that, to describe even part of a fully clothed figure, one must first imagine the whole body naked. It had often amused him as he worked on depictions of wealthy donors, to think of how the artists must have privately seen them as they sketched. It was the same with Ariadne. He knew the form of her arms. Sensed the lie of her thighs as she sat supported on that paint-stained stool. Described, first in chalk and then in paint, the rise of her throat from her cloak, and knew the curve of her belly and the weight of her breasts. Then he shaped and blended these forms differently and by subtle measures to describe what the pull of the earth and the drag of time would do to them.

There was a stillness about her. Sometimes, she scarcely seemed to breathe. As his hands moved quickly from palette knife to brush, it almost seemed as if the image he was creating was more real than the woman who sat in the dimness before him, and that, held within the shadows where he stared, there really was a woman of far greater age. What, after all, was she? Clearly, she was wealthy. The money she had provided in coins of gold was more than he would have ever dared to ask. Clearly, she was also highly-born. Her voice, her manner, her plain but expensive clothes, all spoke of privilege and a kind of fine living—although Ezekiel still struggled to imagine exactly what that living might be. Did she dine at the tables of the highest nobility? Did she and her family sit each Sunday at the high, private balcony of a church whilst her ancestors mouldered in the crypt below? It was almost as if she disappeared from the world when she slipped from his presence—although her face, those eyes, her smile, the limpid curves of her body, reigned stronger than ever in his head.

Of course, the painting was also a deep frustration to him. Not only was he certain that he could never do justice to the image of an Ariadne even with her hair greyed by more than moonlight and her beauty made frail by many extra years, but he was conscious as he had never been in any other task he had performed that a person cannot be captured by colour and shape alone. As well as the silence, the stillness, that emotion which was neither sadness nor happiness, he became increasingly aware as the moon gave way night by night to a pure darkness which seeped across the workroom to fill his canvas, that Ariadne gave off a slight but intoxicating scent. He was reminded of the tang of Grete's breath that he found most desirable in the days of the month before she informed him that they could not sleep as husband and wife. Reminded, too, as the sickle moon thinned to nothing, of the darker smell that followed, which he knew to be the stain of Eve.

Then came a night when there was no moon at all, and the whole of Strasbourg was fallen into blackness, and Ezekiel Morel paced the studio in a kind of anguish, and alone. The dark panel, by now near-complete, but still so unsatisfactory, awaited, taunting him. As did the empty stool by the window. To be so near, and yet not done! Where on earth was she? But Ariadne returned with the moon, and within another few nights the panel was finished, although he insisted she wait a further fortnight for the oils to dry, by which time the moon was full. When she came that final night to collect it, and after he given her cotton-wrapped panel and taken the last of the agreed money, and stood breathing in the last of her presence, he scurried to the window. There she was, moving quick and dark as a bat's shadow before a turn in the street and a twist of the night took her away.

His name was Ezekiel Morel, and he was mostly content with his life and his business, and the strange commission from the woman

9

who had called herself Ariadne soon passed into memory. Still, he found he often went by deviant routes when he finally took the steps down from his workroom at night and headed toward his home and his family. As his work required, he was always on the look out for interesting shapes, figures, features and faces which might be subtly interpolated into the work of some long-dead genius. Not just the beautiful, but the bizarre and the ugly. He wandered beside the darkest canals where slept the dying and the leprous. He risked the attentions of footpads and brigands.

Meanwhile—almost, it seemed, on some quick evening when his back was turned—his daughters grew into young women. Josette discovered a fruit stall in the market run by a young grocer from whom she was particularly keen to make purchases, whilst Julie became unreasonably loyal to the produce of a baker who plied his trade amid the leaning old buildings of Petit France. Ezekiel was happy for his daughters, for these were both good men. When they came to seek his approval for a union of their families, he was surprised at how nervous they both seemed, until he remembered how he had once felt.

Next, Roland was old enough to commence formal training in the workshop, although Ezekiel was clear that he would treat him with no more favour than the other apprentices. Despite the lad's obvious talent, there was something about his manner, an insolence he displayed when running errands or talking to his betters, which Ezekiel felt sure the discipline of work would correct. When he discovered his son daydreaming one hot summer afternoon on the stool by the window, he didn't hesitate strike him hard across the cheek.

With his daughters soon married, and his business well-established, Ezekiel found that he and Grete could afford better lodgings, with bigger windows, and more rooms than they needed, especially as even Roland was rarely present, but out carousing in the bars or whatever else young men now did to waste their money and time. Physically, Roland reminded Ezekiel of how he had looked at that age, whilst the plump, sag-cheeked and bald-headed man he now saw in the mirror above the washing bowl reminded him a little of his old master Nesch—and even to see that peculiar vision, he had to peer and squint. His sight wasn't as good as it had been, nor was his hand so precise. This, he thought, as he instructed the other apprentices to perform work he would once have kept for himself, and avoided climbing the taller ladders in the cathedral for the hurt it brought to his knees, is exactly when I need a son. But Roland rarely attended the workshop. When he did, he was often drunk.

A bad example and a huge disappointment. There was nothing Grete could tell Ezekiel about the lad's delicacy of body or temperament, or the supposedly free spirit of this new age where people talked of the supposed rights of mankind, that would make him change his mind unless and until Roland buckled down. It was as he fell to pondering this and other issues in his workshop one winter evening, sat on that stool by the window in the full fall of the moon when he should have been at work on the head of Saint Anthony that some madman had recently vandalised, that he heard the creak of the street door, and quick patter of footsteps he hadn't heard in twenty years.

"Ezekiel..."

There she was. It could have been the same cloak, but that it was so new, and it was certainly the same face that the hood revealed, framed by the same exquisite fall of golden hair. He stood up, bowed, fumbled an apology for his unpreparedness. His heart was hammering. His head felt light. For all that he thought he'd maintained a clear recollection of Ariadne, he'd forgotten how beautiful she was. She smiled that smile which wasn't quite a smile. Gestured across the crowded workroom.

"You have done well. All those assistants you now have, and two daughters married, and one with a baby and the other with child. A happy marriage yourself, or one that works. And a son...well, at least he's alive and living by his own lights, if not yours. But to be a *réparateur*—a repairer of things, to be busy in your life with simple business of putting beautiful things back to they way they were, or perhaps even adding a little more beauty of your own..."

Ezekiel agreed that he was indeed, blessed.

"I have followed your work. That weeping angel in the chapel of Our Lady of Sorrows in the south aisle of the cathedral. That smiling demon in the church of Madeleine. Both, in their own way, equally moving and superb."

He thanked her, although he could scarcely take in the blaze of whatever she was. Her presence, beauty and scent. The moon was rising now at the window, but there no lines for its light to etch upon her face, no silver for it to touch in her hair. He ventured, in a

11

mumble, that she, too, had been blessed, but that harsh dark in her eyes flared like broken ice.

"Don't use that word about me, Ezekiel," she hissed. "I am as I am, and made as you see me, although that panel you painted has been a kind of comfort. But not enough, I'm afraid. Nothing of anything is ever enough... That is why I need you to paint me again, my head and shoulders as before, but now filled with the burden of all those extra years."

"But that would mean—"

"Exactly. You were kind to me last time, Ezekiel. Perhaps too kind, even if you were also true. You painted me as a woman possessed of the sort of good looks to which those who are rich and fortunate enough may cling even as years start to stretch their skins and douse their spirits. But now there can be no such denial. I want you this time to paint me without beauty and without grace. I want you to paint the half-seeing blur of my eyes and the gleam of my scalp through spiderweb hair and the wheeze of my breathing and the hurt in my bones. I want you to paint me as an old woman, Ezekiel—like those creatures you see late on in the market, muttering between their few teeth as they search for scraps amid the cabbage stalks. The sort that people call hags when they notice them at all."

Ezekiel set to work. He rearranged his life around those evenings, and spoke little to Grete, and never to his son. Ariadne's lack of change over the years seemed far less extraordinary to him than it should. What would have seemed stranger, he realised as he worked on his first sketches in charcoal and chalk that mimicked the moonlight in which she sat, would for her to have appeared to him as the crone he was now required to draw. After all, he had spent his whole life reshaping angels, restoring demons. If Ariadne had developed wings, or grown a halo or sprouted talons, his cause for surprise would have scarcely increased.

He peered up at rain-drooling gargoyles. He examined the ruined faces of beggars in the street. Late at night when he finally returned home, he studied Grete's careworn sags as she lay sprawled and snoring beside him in their marriage bed. Flesh turning to grey as it slid off the bone. Even the secret hair between her thighs wintering to grey. He knew he could not be kind in his depiction of Ariadne this time, and his eye remained true, even if it strained for light and saw the real world less clearly. If anything, the work which he produced scared him more than any painting or torture or damnation he had ever witnessed or repaired. Yet all he was describing were the simple effects of old age.

There is a lunar year as well as a solar one, and Ezekiel wondered if whatever kind of life Ariadne lived was governed by those different seasons which he and no other living man could know. When she left his workroom after these sessions, especially as the moon darkened and the work in all its subtle horror grew near complete, he found himself staring at the window, straining his eyes to watch the retreat of a shadow which could have been nothing more than a fleck of night.

Then came the night when the moon was nothing but a black space set high amid the stars like the bleakest depths of Ariadne's pupils, and he knew she would not come. Still, he went up to his studio as the bells rang and the city gates were shut, and took the near-finished panel out from its hidden corner, set it on its easel, then laid out all the scraps of drawing that accompanied it. He studied them as if with the intention of perhaps adding a few final flourishes to the barely discernible thing that he'd somehow created in paint from time, mortality and the dark. Somewhere far outside, and deep in the still night, he thought he heard a shrill, wracking scream, although it might have been nothing but a fox or a cat, or some other night animal.

Then, far below, he heard the street door bang. Footsteps followed.

"Ariadne?"

But the footsteps were slow, and heavy. The wavering fan of a lantern, and a smell of taverns, long preceded his son's final arrival in the workroom.

"Ah—it's just as I thought."

Roland was dressed, Ezekiel thought, in the most stupidly ridiculous harlequin clothes, all topped by a foppish hat that a drayman would have hesitated to put on a horse. Yet he had the pompous, nosy manner of the worst kind of cleric—the sort who saw evil and pollution everywhere about them except in the mirror. Oh yes, Ezekiel knew about those. Yet he had heard his son loudly proclaim that Reason was now the only God.

"Hiding up here, eh?" he slurred. "Working on some peculiar and doubtless money-making task which glories the natural state of man not at all."

13

As Roland held the lantern high and peered about him as if astonished, it seemed as if he was witnessing the workroom for the first time.

"The money I make, Roland, is the money that puts you in those absurd garments."

It felt good to say that. Too late, though, Ezekiel realised that he had stupidly made no attempt to cover his easel. His son bumbled forward into a worm-corroded statue of Saint Perpetua, nearly removing her miraculously unsevered head, then righted himself with the unsteady ease of a practised drunk.

"What is this thing?" Roland held the lantern so close to the panel that Ezekiel feared he might set the thing alight. "It's horrid."

This was the first time Ezekiel has seen this work so strongly illuminated, and he could see the truth in his son's statement. This was a portrayal of something more than age. There was a malevolent gleam in the old creature's bleared and hooded eyes that he would have sworn the real Ariadne could never possess. Worse still, though, was the way it was mimicked in his son's returning stare.

"And these—what are these?"

Now, he was rummaging through the spill of Ezekiel's nearby sketches, many of which went back to his previous portrait, and described Ariadne not only as she might become, but also as she truly was, and entirely naked of everything but her beauty and grace.

"Ha!" His son's hands were greedy as they ruffled through the sheets. His eyes were greedier still. "Old goat. Old bastard. So this is what you really get up to? Naked as Eve, and twice as dirty. Where's the model, eh?" Roland raised the lantern and peered about him as if another figure really might be there. The light fell on the stool by the window, stretching the shadows of its legs to some spidery thing which crawled across the walls and floor. "These are too good not to have been drawn from life. But then, you always did have a decent hand. At least, when you weren't hitting me with it."

"You don't understand."

"What's there to understand in filth?"

"There are things too strange and dark and wonderful, Roland, for you to ever comprehend with all your talk of science and logic. Creatures, beings of the night, who—"

"Ha! Beings! Creatures! Next thing you'll be telling me she's a succubus—or a vampire come to suck your blood..."

14

Ezekiel made a lunging grab for the papers, but Roland resisted, holding them up beyond his father's reach in the manner of bullies throughout history.

"Come on, then! Dance for your dirt, you grubby old goat! Dance for your stupid vampire whore!"

Although Ezekiel would have denied ever using his hands against his son apart from that one unfortunate occasion, he used them now. Young and easy on his legs as Roland was, he was drunk and short of breath, and lacked his father's sinewy strength. Far more than any wounding words about his son's fashion-sense, it felt deplorably good to strike out with his fists. He found himself filled with a quickness and rage he hadn't known his mind and body still possessed.

The uneven fight was quickly concluded. The bunched sheets of drawings, a hundred different Ariadnes, scattered, and Roland sunk back, his pummelled face askew with blood, anger, hurt. Feeling slick warmth on his knuckles, Ezekiel licked it off.

Roland, wide-eyed, let out a sobbing howl, and stumbled back toward the stairs, the lit lantern he somehow still clutched in his hand catching and changing the expressions of all the many watching saints from glee to horror to sorrow, and, finally, to smirking mirth. Ezekiel slumped down on the dark stool by the dark window as his son's footsteps faded, wondering if things might not have ended better if the lantern had spilled, and they had both gone up in oily smoke.

Just as she had done before, Ariadne returned with the gaining curve of the moon. As before, she offered no apology and Ezekiel sought no explanation for her absence during the darkest time of the month, and soon the ancient thing on the panel was finished and done, although he made her wait until the thing was fully dry before he allowed her to take it.

"Thank you, Ezekiel. You have made me into something even worse than I feared."

"That isn't—"

"But it *is*." She stopped him with her beautiful, mirthless smile. "And you know it to be so. Here..." She held out a bag for him to take. He knew from the feel and the weight of it that, as before, it would be filled with old francs minted with the faces of ancient kings. "This is much less than you deserve."

He bowed his acceptance, grossly uneven though the exchange was. "Can I ask you something, Ezekiel?"

"Of course."

"Have you yet spent the money I gave you twenty years ago?"

He shook his head. He knew he should have done—there had certainly been times when his family or his business needed the money—but...

"No, no. You have no need to offer excuses. In fact, you are very wise." Briefly, her face grew terribly stern. "Keep these coins if you can, Ezekiel. At least, for now. Many things eventually loose their value, but gold is one of the last to do so, no matter what its form. Even, or perhaps I should say, especially, in troubled times. You have heard far clearer than I how people on the streets now talk. The things they now dare to say about the King, and the clergy, and the life they feel forced to live. I do not know what is coming, Ezekiel..." Ariadne paused, and seemed to shiver. The whole room trembled like a wind-blown veil. "But I sense a great storm."

He stood and watched her leave the workroom with the panel clasped beneath her cloak. Listened a while to the fading patter of her footsteps. Breathed slowly so as not to lose the last remains of her intoxicating scent. Then, and although he knew it broke some unspoken part of their agreement, he dashed downstairs as fast as his creaking legs would carry him. The night street was empty, the silver-bright city frozen in sleep. The dazzle of moonlight spread across his eyes as he began to weep.

Life returned to what Ezekiel supposed he must now call normality. Work continued. Apprentices came and went, but none did he trust enough to pass over his business. Father Charbonneau had risen well in the church, and ensured Ezekiel was given the most delicate work in the cathedral that less experienced hands might have ruined. The famous clock, however, was no longer ticking for want of some small part, and the father privately confided as the two men sat in a nearby bar that there was as little money, and almost as much debt, to be found in the coffers of the church as in those of the nation. Ezekiel agreed that the world was going upside down, and wondered aloud if they had moved into an age in which time was governed by the turning of the moon rather than the sun.

Father Charbonneau rubbed his greyed beard and studied Ezekiel oddly. "The world has changed, certainly. But it sounds to me as if you are speaking not of the future, but of the past, and of the kind of old gods our church once fought to destroy. Now, though..." The priest's gaze lowered to his scummed beer. "I fear it is our turn. The new god is called reason, or logic, or some such. But we have both lived longed enough, my old friend, to know that all gods are jealous, and that they are vengeful, and trample and destroy all who do not bow down to worship them."

The stairs up to his workroom were much steeper now, and the rough pine rail beside them had grown polished and dark as mahogany. Winters came and went. The storks left their rooftop nests with their new young, and flew off to some far place which was said to be the Kingdom of Prester John, or even perhaps that of our Lord in Heaven. Certainly, down in these city streets, and even within the great churches Ezekiel saw less and less evidence of Him.

Then, one night, in bed, and at home, he awoke as if disturbed by some dark occurrence. Ariadne? But no. A finger of moonlight probed his sore eyes. The house around him stirred. Timbers wheezed. A baby somewhere was crying. What was it, then? A foul smell, for certain. But that was hardly extraordinary in this increasingly overcrowded city. An intruder? But it felt more to him as if something was missing. He turned to Grete, although he knew how much she would grumble if he awakened her, and saw that she was sprawled oddly. For once, she wasn't even snoring. The sheets around her shone dark.

Roland reappeared for the funeral, and made a speech over the grave which even Father Charbonneau admitted was impressive, for all that it made no mention of God, or Christ, or any of the blessed saints. Grete was, apparently, a model citizen, whose sacrifice was a lesson to all, and a vision of modesty who had never struck out at even the smallest and most innocent creature. Ezekiel's two daughters howled their grief, and his several grandchildren whose names he sometimes struggled to remember howled with them. Only he remained dry-eyed.

Josette's and Julie's families moved in to share Ezekiel's rooms. It made every kind of sense, for both their husband's businesses were struggling, and, after all, what grandparent didn't want to see, and hear, more of their grandchildren? Nevertheless, space and privacy were at a premium. Even when he wasn't at his workshop, Ezekiel often spent his nights wandering the city's chiaroscuro streets. Was

17

life really more violent and treacherous than before, as his daughters warned? Or were these seemingly changes really just a product of the disillusionment of age?

The theatres. The brothels. The people who emerged from either, or both, pyramidal with their huge bellies and incredible clothes. Topped by powdered wigs, birdcage hats, bleached and reddened faces he would have hesitated to use when re-describing the demons in some vision of the lowest, darkest quarters of Hell. The beggars. The street-women. The alleyway boys. The jowling cats and snarling dogs. So many creatures the night conjured as if from nothing, Ezekiel wondered if there were enough left over to fill up the day.

Once, he was knocked sideways as he straddled a puddled gutter and strove to piss away the age-ravaged features of the old man who stared back at him. Just a corpulent guardsman, spilling out from the lit bar opposite, gripping some woman he'd found. Nothing so unusual about that. But the woman was struggling and protesting as he dragged her toward a nearby alley which, on this moonless night, loomed like a well of pure black.

Before he'd had time to think about the wisdom of his actions, Ezekiel grasped after the guardsman's brocade cloak, and said that he should let the woman, who clearly had no desire to do business with him, go. The guardsman snarled and leapt around. In another instant, a sword flashed silver-dark. Ezekiel knew he was supposed to step back, but he felt no inclination to do so. After all, what had he left to loose?

"Come on, then," he muttered. "Kill me if you must."

The guardsman looked puzzled. The point of his sword wavered close to Ezekiel's belly. Then it began to droop. As did the guardsman's grip on the woman, who gasped her thanks before staggering drunkenly back toward the supposed safety of the bar. His face a picture of angry incomprehension, the guardsman uttered a few oaths, then sheathed his sword and stomped off, boots jingling, into the alley's deeper dark.

It could have been the next dawn. It could have been a year or so later. That, for Ezekiel, was how things now were. The sun greyed invisible, and the whole city cloaked in mist as emerging from a dream. Cries and muffled commotions down by the islands of the Ponts Couverts. People running past him in and out of the fog. Doors and windows bursting open. More slowly, favouring the side of his hip that hurt him less in damp weather, Ezekiel followed. Men in a barge were struggling to lift something that was turning beside the weir. Gasps and shouts of horror among the onlookers. Furtive signs of the cross. Calls for a grappling hook, and then for more rope. Finally, the thing was lifted, eyes bulging and the rent in its throat a yawning mouth. The guardsman held high and dripping in the gaining light, caught on the brocade edge of his cloak.

France was in penury for financing a war to give a few malcontents on the far side of the Atlantic independence from the British, and the King had dismissed yet another clutch of ministers, and the Queen was apparently engaged in pretending to be a shepherdess at Versailles. That was, when she wasn't educating her courtiers in the more extreme arts of love as depicted in the gross cartoons available on almost every street corner. Ezekiel could admire the handiwork of these drawing, but otherwise cared nothing for such things.

On many nights, especially the blackest, most moonless ones, he still ranged across Strasbourg like a man possessed. Would have been robbed many times, had he possessed anything worth taking. Instead, he was cursed, threatened, abused. Women, seeing his face at their windows, cried out and covered their faces, or drew their children to their aprons. He sat hunched with beggars beneath bridges. Heard talk there of a dangerous yet wondrous creature who moved amongst their kind like a dark angel when the time came for death. He lay at the edges of fires as their tales dwindled and awoke far beyond dawn, his clothes rigid with frost. Once, a body nearby him failed to stir even as the roar of sunlight deepened. He and the other figures clustered around it in their steaming rags. They prodded it, muttered, wailed. Leaning close, Ezekiel noted the leprous skin, sunken eyes, and the stench that this diseased and shrivelled body must have given off long before it was dead. Noted, too, the scrawny throat with its pinprick rents.

Death in its many guises had always roamed these city streets, and Ezekiel no longer thought it an unwelcome guest. If there were ancient gods as Father Charbonneau claimed, surely this of all deities would outlast the rest? Sometimes, chasing shades within shadows, he thought he was close to some kind of holy state of unknowing. Then, on a cold night so brightly dark that the stars hurt his eyes, he heard from a lanternless alley a scream too feral to be that of a nightbird or cat. He followed it eagerly, and found himself tasting the reek of something strong yet evanescent. He knew he was chasing the smoke of dreams, yet he cried out as he ran until he found himself standing in the courtyard of a small but familiar square on the eastern side of the city, and glimpsed the closing door of a house opposite even as he fought for breath.

No great thoroughfare, but he'd passed through this square many times. Had even paused to drink from this central well. His burning legs dragged him close enough to the house with the closed door for him to note its tallness, and narrowness, and its bolted and shuttered windows, before a restraining pressure like an invisible hand began to lay itself against his chest, making him turn away. Ezekiel limped back across Strasbourg toward his own home, and the ever-anxious enquiries of his daughters, and snatched a few hours uneasy sleep before another day's work as a struggling *réparateur* began.

Ezekiel found himself visiting and re-visiting that resolutely ordinary square. The government might be formally bankrupt and the King in his wisdom might have called and dismissed several Assemblies of Notables, but something like everyday life still continued in this quiet corner of Strasbourg. Maids leaned from windows to beat rugs. The odd carriage came and went. Servant-boys whistled to and from the well with no thought for the Third Estate.

That tall house, distinguished from all the others only by its narrowness and ever-closed shutters, was ignored. Even when you made a considerable effort, it was difficult to stare for long at the place, so Ezekiel found. The action of actually walking to its heavy oak door was almost impossible to think of, let alone perform. Get too close, and the restraining hand which touched you as you gazed at it became a cold fist which closed hard around your heart. Step a little back, though, glance at the place merely sideways and for a moment, and it didn't seem remotely unusual. Nor was it sinister or unkempt. In fact, it was scarcely there at all. Ezekiel found a similar phenomena when he tried asking passing servants, tradesmen and neighbours about its history and inhabitants. A casual question would get a puzzled shrug. Press harder, and people grew uncomfortable. They looked at him like he was some terrible, mad, old man—or worse—and walked quickly off.

Times were hard, and the summer grew hot, and the city buzzed with rumour like the pall of flies which hung over it. Even Ezekiel, as he sat up in his workroom amid his ruined saints and abandoned angels was drawn back downstairs one morning by a particularly loud commotion. People were marching, shouting, singing. For once, they seemed happy. He gathered that a prison in Paris, known as the Bastille, had been broken into, that its governor had been killed and his severed head paraded on a spike through the streets, and that a few inmates had been released. Gathered, although he struggled to understand why, that this was a cause for great celebration.

Other celebrations were to follow as the King and Queen were brought to Paris, and the Rights of Man were declared. Shops in Strasbourg were broken into. Markets looted. There were street-corner speeches, and a great deal of fist-waving. Even with the window shut fast up in his workroom to keep in the precious scents of linseed and wood-shavings, Ezekiel could hear the roar of voices, and sound of shattering glass and the whinny of terrified horses.

Still, all was not to the bad. In fact, far from it, as a resolutely cheerful Father Charbonneau insisted to Ezekiel the following winter as they shared a hugely expensive beer sat at their old table in what had once been their usual bar. Things had certainly been difficult for the clergy, and many churches had been desecrated, but now the First Estate had voted to join the National Assembly and were officially employees of the nation, it would all settle down. The abolishment of tithes and the nationalisation of church property were simply the political means of returning to the precepts of fairness and frugality which Christ himself had taught. Give it a few more months, a year at most, and things would be back to a better kind of normality. And he was, of course, deeply conscious of the fees that Ezekiel was owed, and the problems with damp penetration and woodworm infestation which needed addressing behind the cathedral's high altar and in the dean's aisle.

But the nights now blazed with fire. Even that quiet square in the eastern side of the city, the one that had seemed so far away from these troubled times, was now permeated by the reek of smoke. The King and Queen had been arrested and hauled back to Paris from a place called Varennes. Ezekiel and his family had no money, and no means to pay for things—at least, if you discounted his hidden horde—and were forced to scrabble and barter like everyone else, for all the National Assembly's promises that things would soon get better.

Ezekiel kept working on the few commissions he still had, even though his daughters told him it was dangerous to be seen entering churches, and, despite Father Charbonneau's promises, he wasn't getting paid. He'd lived a long life, and things had been hard before, and he was not the sort of man to let the silly posturing of a few self-proclaimed men of the people get in his way. To his mind, the fact that his own son had returned from Paris to play a leading role in the so-called Revolutionary Committee which now supposedly ran this city said all that needed to be said. Still, he knew that something more than the passage of mere events was gripping France on the morning when he entered that quiet square where servant-boys had ceased to whistle and maids no longer beat rugs to find shattered windows, and that something foul-smelling had been cast down into the well. What dream, idea or philosophy, he wondered, could require the pollution of something as simple and wholesome as fresh water?

When he forced himself to stare up at the tall, narrow house whose blank gaze he now avoided, he was shocked to discover how easy it was. It was even more shocking to take several more steps towards it, and see that some of its shutters were missing, that its heavy door hung askew. A man in a dream, or a man who at least wished he was dreaming, he stood right before it, and felt none of the hidden mystery of old. The sideways door, he saw, had a sign affixed to it which announced that the building was now the property of the city. Stepping inside, he heard a baby crying and smelled sour human reeks.

It was, or had been, a fine enough house. A broad, decent stairway. Floors of good oak or flagged stone. He jumped when a child pushed by him. Jumped again when he peered around a doorway and saw a toothless old woman sat in a rocking chair with a tricolor cockade stuffed into her greasy bonnet. Had Ariadne really lived here? It seemed incredible, impossible. And, if she had, where was she now? Ezekiel crept. He wandered. He explored. The small back yard was unsanitary and disgusting. Children, or quite possibly adults, had scratched and scrawled their names across the oak panelling of the main hall. Then, beneath the stairway, he found a less obvious door. It was heavy, and well-made. Would have been well-locked, too, and seemingly from the inside, before its mechanisms had been splintered apart. To his surprise, he found a nearby flint

22

and lantern which, unlike most things in this city, actually worked. He descended the stone stairway beyond with a sinking feeling, but no fear.

A kind of cellar, crypt or chapel. It could have been all of these things. Dry and quiet. Cool in summer. Mild in winter. Heavy-pillared. Gracefully stone-arched. In the centre, a kind of platform. Alter? Table? Bed? But of course, the citizens had been here before him, and the place reeked of urine, and there were more of those scratches and scrawlings that deface the city as a whole. The only reason someone didn't live down here, or keep pigs the way they now often did in churches, was because of a small but lingering sense of trespass. He searched in vain, though, for any evidence of struggle. Saw, as well, that there was no sign of his two panels, although he noted two empty alcoves, and then a third, into which a final part of his triptych would have fitted.

Ezekiel re-ascended the stairway, spirits somehow lighter than they had been in many months. He sensed not that Ariadne had been destroyed, but that she had—very wisely—fled. After all, and just as his own daughters were always telling him, Strasbourg was no longer safe. Least of all for anyone who might be perceived to be noble, beautiful or refined. He was met in the main hallway by a varied group of concerned and angry local citizens, who wished to know exactly what he thought he was doing wandering about what they now thought of as their property, even if the private ownership of anything was now technically regarded as theft. He mumbled his excuses as their blows started to rain down on his head. He was he supposed, as he picked himself up bloodied from the cobbled square outside, lucky to have escaped the place with his life, or not to have been thrown down that ghastly well.

The following spring, a strange, new, tree-like structure began to grow beneath his workshop window in the old parade ground. It was called a guillotine and it was modern, humane and egalitarian like all creations of this new, enlightened age. Strasbourg's greatest pride in all its long and distinguished history, however, was that it had originated the new song called the *Marseillaise* which everyone was singing, at least when they weren't rioting for food. Churches had reopened their doors as new Temples of Reason. It had been some time since Ezekiel had seen Father Charbonneau, or any other man who dared to call himself priest. Only the storks, with their clumsy-graceful dancing and clacking as they mated, seemed unmoved by all the changes. At his daughter's begging, he removed the faded sign from his lower doorway which announced his name and trade. Even then, and because of the taint of their association, he began to fear that his family were no longer safe.

Another winter. As ever, the storks fled south. But now there was no Christmas, for this was Year One in the New Revolutionary Calendar, and the month in which the King was executed was named Pluviôse, or "rainy". This was, or would have been, the very season and twenty years since Ariadne's last visit to his workshop. In other times, Ezekiel might have hoped for her return. But not now. France was at war, Marat had been murdered, Lafayette had fled to Austria and no one was to be trusted. Committees of Public Safety were established in every town to ensure that the revolution continued along its glorious, inevitable path, and the guillotine in the old parade ground square, which had previously been an occasional curiosity, began to see frequent, regular work. After all, Ezekiel reasoned as he heard the brief hush and slide of metal which punctuated the jeering and cheering, the theatres were shut, the bars were dry, and the new Temples of Reason did often still reek of pig.

One morning, as he struggled to get his gluepot fire lit with the remains of a cherub's leg and some saint's fingers, he heard a particularly loud commotion. Against the prompting of his better judgement, he cleared a space in his frosted window to look down. Father Charbonneau was far thinner than Ezekiel remembered, and he was mostly naked, and someone had hacked off his beard. Still the old priest kept his dignity as he was dragged from the tumbrel and across the frozen snow towards the marsh of mud and blood which surrounded the guillotine. Then, up on the platform, he raised his voice loud and clear enough to reach even Ezekiel's faded hearing as he gave thanks for his life, and called for God's mercy on all involved in these deeds. Ezekiel, too, gave thanks that his old friend died quickly, and hadn't been torn limb from limb by the mob, or cast tied upon the river, or stoned like some ancient prophet, or buried alive, or slowly roasted on a spit. He turned back to his beloved workroom for a moment, paused, then hobbled as quietly and quickly as he could down the stairs.

Although both their husbands had been conscripted, he found Josette and Julie and their children in the remains of their apartment, which they now had to share with several other families. They shook their heads at him when he whispered his plan. Not because they doubted the wisdom of fleeing across the Rhine to Saxony, but because they knew it would be vastly expensive. How could they of all people possibly afford the necessary bribes?

New snow had fallen in a deep, white layer on the night of their escape. Sounds fell dead. Fires died. Water froze in kettles. As he stood with his family in the wood where they had gathered just outside the walls of the city, Ezekiel looked up toward the deep sky, and was pleased to see barely a sliver of moon. The cart arrived. He helped lift their few belongings.

"You must come." It was Josette—no, it was Julie: all these years, and he sometimes still struggled to tell his daughters apart. He shook his head and stepped back. He watched the cart creak slowly off, filled with the framed faces of everyone he loved.

The last of the moon had clouded over when he returned to the gates of Strasbourg, and the citizens he had paid to stay at their posts quietly let him in through a side door. He walked alone though the dark, white, empty streets, and climbed to his workroom with a vigour he hadn't felt in years. It was good to know he had something he needed to do again. The precious fire lit with more holy limbs, relics and fragments of scared image, his fingers finally unfrozen, Ezekiel set to work.

He had found, seasoned and set aside the third panel to this triptych long ago. Now, he sketched with a fever. His body still shivered but his hands remained sure. Chalk. Charcoal. Gesso. Precious supplies which he'd hoarded for this precise moment and task. Sometimes, he would glance over to the empty stool beside the window, but he didn't need Ariadne to paint the thing he now had to paint. After all, she was beautiful, immortal, inviolate. And what he was creating was a grinning mask of death. Then came the oils. He was rushing things, he knew, and old master Nesch would have been horrified, but tonight the paints had a will of their own. A worm-rotted mask of oblivion stared back at Ezekiel in a leering, welcoming yawn. He wasn't painting Ariadne, but this world, this city, and as red dawn rose over the snow-clad city and touched the glistening horror he'd created, he felt that his work was almost done. One last shape or stroke, perhaps. But what?

25

Then, as he stood at his easel and his palette knife wavered, he heard the sound of his door being dragged open from the street. Then footsteps. His heart leapt. But they were too many, and too heavy, and the rising sun was already far too bright. The door to his workroom burst open in a fug of humanity and noise. Saints fell. Crucifixes were broken. The sagging floor, which had surely never supported so many bodies, groaned. Ezekiel still gripped his palette knife, but many hands were upon him. The thing was torn from his fingers and skittered away.

He had heard that a man called Roland was in the city, but he had not believed that this Roland whose deeds he had heard of could really be his son. But there he stood, right in the middle of this group of all ages, sexes and builds which might have made a fine crowd for the background in a crucifixion. Roland was plumper now, which was a rare thing in these times of scarcity. He was also what might have been called well-dressed, even if his choice of clothing was predictably garish. He wore what seemed to have been a bishop's robe, although the crosses and symbols of piety had ripped off and replaced by emblems of revolutionary zeal. The ornate silver staff he was using to help support his considerable weight was undoubtedly a bishop's crosier, and many of the rings that he wore also looked to be ecclesiastical in origin—great gold things which Ezekiel felt the smart of as he was struck hard across the face.

"Here you are, old man!" Roland proclaimed breathlessly, although, even with his strong theatrical bent, he couldn't manage to inject his words with very much surprise. "Skulking and hiding, creating your disgusting fairy tale images as your co-conspirators flee to the enemies of the Republic."

"Your sisters, their children. Are they—"

The hard slap, although this one was less accurate, came again.

"There are no such relationships in this new republic! We are all only sons and daughters of Liberty. And do you think us so foolish, so drowsy, as to let such stupid plans succeed?"

Did that mean Josette, Julie and their families had been arrested? By now, they should have been close to the Rhine, if not already on the barge which would take them across it to safety. If not, as he was kicked down the stairs, he would see them again soon enough. The citizens of this new state loved their trials almost as much as they

26

loved their executions—at least, as long as there was a guaranteed guilty verdict.

He was put in heavy iron shackles and thrown along with many others into the cellars of the customs house. The smell was considerable. High, barred widows half-blocked by the snow gave in a grey, pestilential light. There was no food and no toiletry arrangements, only a little disgusting water to drink. Ezekiel peered and wandered, dragging his chains. Pleading hands rose toward him. People moaned. Pleaded. Wept. A vision of Hell, he wondered? But the grainy light from those windows was unremitting, and surely Satan and his minions would be better organised than this? At intervals, the top door was thrown open and new prisoners cast in. Each time, he studied them anxiously. But still no sign of his family. Had they really been captured, or had Roland simply been bragging without good reason, as he'd often done before everything changed? This was, Ezekiel thought as he hunched back against the freezing stone, a strange place for a man to feel hope.

The day dragged by. Faintly from outside came the sounds of everyday life, which now meant little else but a great deal of shouting. Ezekiel tried to consider who might have betrayed him, but the possibilities were too many. He tried to comfort himself instead with visions of this family on a barge, crossing the Rhine's winter-sluggish waters. He'd never thought of Saxony as a land of great beauty, but it seemed that way to him now. He saw sun-pierced clouds and the flower-threaded paths along which his family would walk, in a place where the old calendar still worked and the months didn't have ridiculous names.

As the shadows changed and the afternoon grew on, Ezekiel noticed a stir in a bundle of rags in a far corner that he'd previously assumed to be a corpse. On the horrible offchance that it might be one of his family, he hauled his chains over to inspect it. He picked up a filthy corner of the cloth, which seemed to have adhered to the skin beneath, and a sweet, sickly reek of burnt flesh arose. Pitiful. Another example of the revolution's bright zeal. He'd turned away to leave the thing to die when he heard it mutter something, and turned back.

"Ez—ee—kiel...?"

The voice was slurred. The face which raised itself from the deepest shadow, a mess of sores and blisters.

"Ariadne?" he breathed. "It can't be."

"There are many things," it sighed, falling back, "that now are, that can't be."

He looked around, then shuffled closer.

"What happened?"

"Give me peace," she muttered drawing herself in so that once again she could have been a corpse, or a mere heap of rags. "Soon it will be night..."

Ezekiel waited. Like a tide slipping between rocks, the darkness pooled first in the deeper spaces. Then, its pools widened and joined as light threaded back from the high, barred windows. The cellar dimmed. Its horrors grew less substantial. Even the crying and moaning diminished. Soon, there was little of anything to be heard or seen, as night spread its blessing.

He told Ariadne why he was here, inasmuch as he could understand. But, after all, Roland was right—he was a traitor to his fellow citizens, a worshipper of ancient idols, and due whatever punishment he was given. Not that it mattered. Not that he cared. That his family weren't here, that they might have made it to freedom across the Rhine, was the sole rock he had left to cling to...

Now that it was fine and fully dark, he sensed Ariadne shift herself a little closer to him. She gave wheezing gasps. Her breath bubbled. Beneath the stink of ruined flesh, like a ghost of a ghost, that deeper, softer scent he could never properly recall when it wasn't there, yet always associated with her, still lingered.

"What happened to me isn't so very different," she whispered. "All of us in this place probably thought that history would leave us unscathed."

"But—"

"Yes. There are many buts, aren't there? You found my old house, didn't you? But you kept away. If you did break our bargain, my dear, sweet Ezekiel, it was only by a very little. But others are different to you, and the world to which you and I belong is disappearing. When I left this city and found a place where I imagined I could sleep my way through this storm, I thought I was being wise and sensible and cautious. But I had underestimated how much and how rapidly people can change. Once, not so very long ago, the wine the priests raised in their chalices truly did turn to blood, and the images in your antique panels showed something close to reality. People *believed*, Ezekiel. But now..." She paused. Gave a ticking swallow. "I was stupid—stupid to imagine these new citizens would respect the supposed sanctity of a family crypt and not break it open and drag me and all the rest of its supposed treasures into the searing daylight."

"What have they charged you with?"

"Does that matter? Once, I suppose, they might have called me an enchantress or harpy or she-devil or fairy. Now, all they need to say of someone is that they look suspicious."

"Can't you—"

"Can't I *what*? Grow wings? Walk through these walls? Just to shake off these horrid irons would be something..."

Silence fell again between them. Ezekiel wondered if he should tell Ariadne he'd been at work on the third part of her triptych. But she sensed that she knew already, just as she knew many other things about him. Her mind, like her gaze, was a dark well into which he could feel himself falling. And in that well, especially on this moonless night, lay an even deeper pit of hunger.

He felt her thoughts, vivid as ink, trickle amid his own. Heard her voice whisper to him, although the sound didn't touch his ears. *As you are, Ezekiel, I once was,* she said. *At least, I lived in light and slept when it grew dark, and knew how to heat water on a fire and carry a bucket, and which mushrooms to pick when I was sent out through the city gates each morning into the river meadows.* Ezekiel saw a proud, turreted city with castellated walls which wasn't Strasbourg. Heard cocks crowing. Dogs barking. Street sellers shouting their wares in a language which wasn't French. Saw a young, startlingly beautiful girl with tied-up blonde hair and a grubby servant's apron wandering down the cobbles, distracted by the crowds and the sun, and carrying a linen-covered wicker basket. *People at the great stone place called Skala where I served called me Ari, but I knew my true name was Ariadne, which was strange in this city of Halkas, Katarzynas and Grazynas. So I always knew that I was chosen for something, and that I was different. As for what I had been chosen for...I didn't greatly care or understand. After all, I was Ari and I was young, and why should I?*

Then Ari was in a fine room, and a fine-looking man was seated at its far end. He beckoned her forward. She curtsied, obeyed. The man's name, Ari already knew, was Hasan, and he was the master of

29

Skala, and all who lived there. He bid her stand before him, cupped her chin and carefully turned her face this way and that, much as one might inspect a precious vase for flaws. He seemed to find none. He smiled.

It was late and the room was heavy-curtained. The fire brought a sweet scent of applewood as he stroked the spun gold of her hair and bid her to lift her limbs and turn in a slow ballerina dance. Then, in his queer, light voice, he instructed her to kneel. She nodded, stooped without question. A silver knife lay beside on a small table, along, warm as the sun in this firelight, with a copper bowl. The man called Hasan bared the left ruff sleeve of his shirt to the elbow, raised the knife, and cut a long, deep incision. He caught the flow in the bowl, and, even without his saying, Ari knew that she should drink. She did so. Easily. Unquestioningly. It filled her head with a confused blur of memories. It tasted salt, surprisingly cold, and made her think of oceans she had never seen. When she had finished, Hasan smiled once more and smeared the blood on her lips with his thumb and told her that she was now truly Ariadne. That she was blessed and they were alone and together for eternity.

So that was who I was. That was what I'd become. Not Ari—who knew how to bark at dogs so they ran away from her, and where to hit nuisance boys—but Ariadne, who grew a fever, and lay in the dark place that Hasan had made for her, afire with a hunger which has never left me since. This man who wasn't a man, who called himself Hasan, he thought he made me as he wanted. Chosen me through hand-picked generations of the faces, races and bodies of servants like a thoroughbred mare. Thought he'd made me in the image of another, long-lost Ariadne, that I was a mirror held to a mirror in the glory of an always-dark place. But I wasn't. Couldn't. The ancient clothes he made me wear. The languages no-one now used he tried to get me to speak. I sometimes wondered if even the first real Ariadne I saw sometimes in the bleak hope of his eyes had ever been the creature he wished her to be. Wondered, as well, why Hasan was alone but for me of all his kind, although I think I soon came to understand that better.

We are predators, Ezekiel. We hunt. We feed. And what predator, be it of night, day, air, land or sea, has ever wanted competition? Hasan took me out with him. We bathed together in the glorious pools of the night and our fabulous needs. He taught me how to

30

stalk, and who to choose. How to feed without killing—or, at least, only killing occasionally when the need reached its absolute peak. For a while ... I wouldn't say I was happy. But I was what I was, and so was he. And, if we were alone, and this was it—well, I decided, so be it. There were joys be found of which little Ari would never have dreamed. I tried to become the Ariadne Hasan wanted. But if he was *alone*—how, and by whom, had he been created? And why, and for what? Neither, when he spoke of lost things and ages long ago, did I believe him.

I became a wild thing, then, Ezekiel. Cantankerous and dangerous and terrible. I experimented. I took risks. I explored all the ways and means of the flesh, both of the dead and the living. I did things which now shame me. Things which would have caused the once-living Ari to make the sign of the cross before her chest and call me a demon. There never seemed to be an end to anything. Not the darkness. Nor, of course, my hunger. Once or twice, just to show that I could, I walked through fires or flung myself off buildings, and the remains I dragged back to Hasan were like a cat with a ruined mouse in its mouth, except the mouse was also me.

Perhaps it was as simple as my needing to prove to him that I wasn't what he thought—that I wasn't his Ariadne. But there always seemed to be something else beneath all of this. Beneath Hasan's smiles and his easy grace and his good manners and his caution and all the exquisite things he had given me. The place we lived in, Skala, was a castle more than a house, rising high of cliffs above the other roofs of the city. Heavy-walled, with battlements, embrasures and arrow-slits. A maze of a place, indeed, with passageways winding within its walls, hidden rooms, blocked doorways, dangerous dead-ends and surprising perspectives. Hasan's control over Skala was great, and people outside thought him a distinguished, if eccentric, nobleman. But now he had made me Ariadne, and I was no longer weak. Nor had I ever been stupid. I unravelled skeins of history from ancient books. I turned over old stones and studied their messages. I questioned those who dared to answer me. I discovered things Hasan would never have wanted me to know. But above all, and night by night, I explored Skala. The barriers he put up which would have left destroyed the minds of others meant nothing to me. Down and down, I went. Deeper and deeper. Stairwell after stairwell. Hallway after hallway. Until the passageways became tunnels

31

and the tunnels became caves cut in bare rock, and the time of the outside world, if there even still was such a thing, no longer had any meaning. A dripping place. A place so dark it hurt even my eyes to see. A place where blood had been spilled for so long that I could feel the very stone screaming. Here, there was not Hasan. Here, there was not Ariadne, or Skala, or this city, or kingdom. But there was something which was at the root of all that we were, and it was horrible beyond words, and ancient beyond measuring...

There were no visions now. There was nothing, and Ariadne's voice was a choked whisper. This, in the hurt of her heart and the tides of her blood, was the black core of the dark sun which she now orbited. Far away now, perhaps. But never gone. So powerful that it rendered meaningless all distinctions between good and bad, between God and the Devil, between life and death. Ezekiel could feel its pull, as well, even as the part of him that knew life struggled not to. For a moment beyond measure, both he and Ariadne were teetering on the lip of something worse than oblivion. Then, by slow degrees, they began to rise back to the real world of this Strasbourg cellar with its stink and pain and horror and history. He would never have thought that such a place could feel so life-affirming.

"So there you are, Ezekiel. Now you know the little I know, but perhaps at least understand why I fled Hasan and the great city of Warsaw two whole centuries gone, and have lived—hid, you might say—alone in my quiet house in Strasbourg." Now, although a murmur that broke through cracked lips, she really was speaking. "I can't say that I haven't killed. In fact, I can claim little of anything, least of all any kind of forgiveness. But I have tried to keep to the pathways which led to those who might almost welcome my embrace. Or..." the longest pause— "...need or deserve it."

The scent she gave off was stronger now. Her breathing also. If she really had been a woman, Ezekiel might almost have thought she was inflamed with passion. But he knew what it was. Knew her, in that moment, almost as well as she knew him. Knew, above all, the pain of her hunger.

"Have me," he muttered. "Have me now."

"Don't say that, Ezekiel..." But she was drawing closer.

"What have I got left to loose?"

"Your family, Ezekiel." He felt the quickening of her breath against his face. The crawl of her hands. "You said so yourself."

"Roland told me they'd already been captured. Which means—"

"Means they'll be brought back here to Strasbourg—brought to trial as you will, and held to account. If you can hold on, Ezekiel, if you can survive this night, there's still a chance."

"I'm just an old man. But..."

Hope again. That thing that reappeared like bad genie, long after it should have turned to dust. And Ariadne was close to him, her chained and ruined body embracing his, and somewhere within those stinking rags was the thing of terror, power and beauty and power she could still become. All it needed was a just little of his blood. He could feel his cock hardening as it hadn't done in years. Could feel the birdcage flutter of her lungs. Could feel her strange lust entwining with his own. Could smell her dark feral scent. This was almost like the furtive negotiations he'd witnessed in dark back alleys, or that he and Grete had engaged in before they married when he was still young. Yes, but no. Do, but don't. An impossible dance.

"It's been so *long* since I've fed, Ezekiel," she drawled, clotted and slow. "I fear I couldn't stop."

The little death and the big death—perhaps they weren't so very different?

"You have to help me in this..." Her voice now a spitting whisper. "...if we are both to survive."

Burnt, slippery twigs, he felt the fingers of her left hand entwine his own. *Now that I am weak, Ezekiel, you must be strong. If we are both to last this night, you must make me stop before the darkness closes over you—break my fingers when you still can...* Then, in a hot spill of glistening drool, her lips were on his throat. He gasped at the pinprick tickle of her teeth. Cried out when the moment of puncture came. Ariadne was every saint and devil incarnate—she was his darkest lust and purest aspiration. He was no longer Ezekiel Morel, one-time family man and *réparateur* who'd lived in the great city of Strasbourg. He was the sacrifice. She was the god.

Already, he could feel the darkness of his submission spreading. In all his life, he had never wanted anything so much. He'd imagined this moment as many things over the years. As a consummation, as an instant of falling, or sheer, blinding terror—or even as something obscene. But now he felt it for what it really was, he was amazed at its ease: it was simply a matter of letting go. But he mustn't. Couldn't. Butterflies of impossible light fluttered before his eyes. His whole body was softening, collapsing. Ariadne's need and her will to consume him were overwhelming. Not just his blood, but his soul and his memories and everything he was. Still, a small part of him was aware of the man he had once been—a man would never turn his back on his family when they might be alive. If he was going to stop Ariadne from destroying him—if he was going to step back from the edge of everything and see another dawn—it would have to be now.

His fingers, arthritic but strong as winter roots, found the thin shape of her smallest finger and began to bend it back. The pulse of her feeding—weakening in him, strengthening in her—scarcely changed. He pushed harder, felt something give. Like a river blocked by an obstacle, Ariadne's need churned and billowed. Then it flooded on.

There was little will—there was little of anything—left in Ezekiel now. Thinking of Grete, although he knew Grete was long dead, he drew the next finger back in a single quick lunge. This time, the obstacle blocking the river's dark flow was larger. He felt the suction of Ariadne's lips briefly weaken. Heard her give, like a sleeper stirring in a dream, a surprised grunt. Now, although he doubted he still had the strength, he took her index finger and broke that as well, and felt the darkness tremble as he heard the bone snap. The thing that was against him hissed and writhed, trying to break free of the pain without letting go. This wasn't Ariadne. This was something wild and ugly. It was only when he broke the last finger that he felt its will weaken and was able to shove the thing away and let it crawl, half-sated like some wounded spider, back into the farthest shadows where it belonged.

Tired, shivering, dizzy, depleted, Ezekiel sat waiting for another dawn. When his fingers explored his throat, all they found were two tiny indentations. As the meticulous daylight slowly revealed the scene in the custom's house cellar, what had happened already seemed vaguer than a dream.

"Ariadne?"

The dark heap didn't stir.

Then the citizen guards returned and—thank the pure spirit of Reason!—there was a little mouldy bread to go with this morning's filthy water, although Ezekiel found he wasn't hungry despite his empty stomach. We could be kept down here for days, he thought. Or years. By the time they finally bring us to what they call justice, we'll be pleading for the scaffold. But then, as the fighting over the water and bread lessened, the guards produced more chains and, with the tongue-protruding concentration of a child collecting daisies, looped the prisoners together one by one. Those who didn't stand up promptly were kicked. Those who still didn't move were struck with iron batons, just to check that they were dead.

Ezekiel found himself standing in the line between an old woman with a missing arm and a mumbling young man with a lost, red-eyed expression whom he was almost sure he'd known as a priest. Looking back into the dim cellar, he saw one of the guards stride over to its furthest corner and lift his boot toward a last pile of rags. Ariadne raised herself just before the boot connected and stood bent with chained hands raised to shield her face. Her left hand was ruined mess, sharp bones jutting out forward and back like broken claws, and the rest of her looked almost as dreadful. It was hard to tell where the burned flaps of skin ended and the tatters of whatever she had been wearing began. Wrinkling his nose and muttering his disgust, the guard linked her shackles to the rest. Then, in a puzzling act of charity, he extricated an old cape from a nearby corpse, laid it across her shoulders, and pulled up the hood to cover her blistered face.

Urged, yelled at and prodded, the line of prisoners shuffled into the surprising light of a city still cloaked in purest white. Ezekiel had to squint and blink away tears. The old woman in front of him stumbled and was half-dragged on through the snow. He couldn't imagine what Ariadne was feeling. Scarcely knew what he felt himself. People emerged from their houses to jeer them on. Snowballs and frozen lumps of horse dung were thrown. But still no sign of Josette, Julie or their children.

Then they were in the square which housed the structure which had been known throughout the rest of its long life as the Cathedral of Our Lady, and was now the Chief Temple of Reason, and also Palace of Justice, for the new Department of Alsace in the Republic of France. The many buildings which it dwarfed seemed to shrug their icicled shoulders at these events. Apart from some new flags and a little graffiti and a few broken windows, they were little changed. The thing about life, Roland supposed, was that it went on no matter what.

Just as always, Ezekiel felt his soul lift as he entered the echoing inner space beyond the cathedral's west door. Many of the statues were covered, and most of the crosses and other sacred symbols which could be easily reached had been removed. But the rood screen still rose before the transept like a glorious gateway in wood and gold, and the glass apostles still blazed. The building had kept its dignity, and he was pleased to see how much of his own handiwork was still in place. At a cursory glance, with its sheeted saints and corner piles of stacked panels and rolled tapestries, the great edifice might have been prepared for nothing more than a vigorous spring clean.

The famous clock, though, remained silent. It had stopped with the skull-face of death emerged from his dark cavity, and the golden wings of the crowing cockerel were clotted with what might have been rust, or feathers, or blood. The faces of the many onlookers who spat at and cursed the prisoners as they processed along the nave had something of death about them as well, although it was hard to place. A greeny-greyness beneath the eyes, perhaps? A pallor of the lips? Something deathly, too, about the citizen judges who sat at the long high table before the rood screen. Or perhaps they were merely tired and bored.

This pre-trial ceremony really was very much like a service of old. The same bowings and shufflings. The same moments of sacred hush. All that was lacking was some incense to spice the reek of unwashed humanity. Then, just as always, something very much like a hymn was sung.

Arise, children of the Fatherland
The day of glory has arrived!
Against us tyranny
Raises its bloody banner...

As the *Marseillaise* rang out beneath the great stone arches Ezekiel saw that many of his fellow prisoners also raised their voices. Not, he sensed, out of fear of not doing so, but from pure belief. Then the Chief Prosecutor emerged, striding forth in his elaborate robe and glittering silver staff, and it was soon clear to Ezekiel that Roland's many nights spent at the theatre hadn't gone to waste.

Here was the man of the hour, and of the people. Even before a verdict was pronounced, the citizens were roaring their decision from the aisles. A false look, a wrong word, a questionable association—these were all that were now needed, but Roland made sure there was always more, and roused his audience to new heights of outrage through well-orchestrated call and response. An inappropriate pair of shoes. A too-hesitant offer of hospitality to a group of sans-culottes. What might have seemed little things became large.

Strasbourg had always been a city in a hurry, so there was no piffling about with allowing these miscreants to await their fate on some other day. Far better, so much more humane, to have them immediately borne to the guillotine. There was much scurrying at the back of the cathedral as citizens hurried to follow the tumbrel on its short journey, then returned to report on how things had gone. All in all, Ezekiel could well understand why so many citizens had become addicted to this whole spectacle, even to the want of sleep and food.

It was already noon and his thoughts were lost when he felt a sudden release of his chains. Light-headed and light-bodied, he was dragged up towards the raised platform beneath the great, dead clock where the accused were required to stand. It was a shock, though, to see that the sheeted easel from his workroom had already been placed there as evidence, and then to hear his son pronounce his name.

"Morel—yes Morel! That's right... For this man who stands before us, accused of the most heinous crimes is, or was, my father."

Astonished gasps. A few citizens who'd been heading out through the west door to follow the tumbrel's latest journey crowded back. Then, reaching to a side-table, Roland silently handed a sheaf of papers to the judges. Their effect, as the pages were fought over, grabbed and passed down into the hands of the watching crowd, was profound. There were horrified gasps. Some of the more sensitive citizens, who had surely seen worse things than some chalk, ink and pencil sketches of a beautiful woman naked—and wasn't Liberty herself bare-breasted?—cried out or swooned. But such was people's need to be shocked, that the drawings soon ended up in shreds.

"I know, I know..." Roland said, rapping his staff and nodding in horrified agreement. "These things are decadent. They are ugly. Above all, they are un-revolutionary. And to think that they came from the mind and hands of this sorry old man. It beggars belief. Yet it is true..." He strode up to Ezekiel. "Do you dare deny it?"

Ezekiel tried to move his mouth and found that nothing would come out. Instead, he shook his head. Then the aisles of the great building were filled with a vast sea-roar of disbelieving horror as Roland ripped off the sheet which covered the easel to reveal the panel beneath. Even to Ezekiel, and especially in the bright glare of this daylight, the thing looked ghastly. It was death, but something more than death. It grinned at you with terrible, knowing intimacy. It drew your eyes as you tried to look away.

Roland, who knew when eloquence was pointless, simply stood there waiting, and his words now seemed oddly redundant even when he started to speak. For here was a man, his very own father, who had not only consorted with the church and all its ridiculous ceremonies and superstitions, but had entered a world were the light of modern reason had no place or purpose. Why, he not only painted such obscenities, but even claimed that he consorted with these creatures of darkness, which danced naked on midnight hilltops and slipped through windows to bother decent citizens in their beds.

The cries of *behead him* were getting louder. Even the judges were joining in. This certainly wasn't the trial Ezekiel had been anticipating. Dreamy lightness, almost an exultancy, began to grow in his head. He'd been expecting to be convicted of helping his family flee France, but it all seemed to have come down to this last panel of his Ariadne triptych...He'd heard that real artists, proper painters, would die for the sake of their work. As a practical man, he'd always doubted such sentiments. Now, though, he would have done so happily. If only he could first know if his family were safe...

"You're right," he croaked. Not particularly loudly, but the crowd had an instinct for the last words of the accused, and grew silent. "Right about everything. I abhor the revolution. I worship the King. No, I worship God, even though I know he no longer exists. As for my family—well, at least apart from my model citizen son—I corrupted them all with my reactionary ideas. They were innocent, they knew Reason. They craved equality. They believed in the Rights of Man. But I forced them to follow the dark ways of which you have now heard, and seen, so much. Forced them, entirely against their own will, to forgo their patriotic duty and leave this great country and accept the terrible embrace of the enemies of France, who—"

"Enough!" A slap rang hard across his face.

At least, he thought, I still have the power to annoy my son. But Roland soon recovered his composure, and turned to the crowd.

"You see—not only has this man striven all his life to destroy the forces of enlightenment. He has conspired to destroy his—and my own—family, as well..."

The citizens settled a little. In truth, they had been looking forward to seeing this old man sent off to be beheaded, and for a fresh counter-revolutionary to be called to justice, but Roland's performance this morning had been exemplary. They knew they were in good hands.

"Bring forth the evidence!" He banged his silver staff. "Bring it forth now." Suddenly, he looked close to tears. "For this is what this old man has done to all that I once loved..."

Two citizens emerged through what had once been chancel door, dragging two stained and heavy sacks. When they shook them out, half a dozen or so roughly roundish objects tumbled out across the tiled space between the nearest onlookers and the judges at their dais. Without realising he had even left his platform, and encountering no resistance as he did so, Ezekiel found he was crouched among them, and raising them one by one. What had once been the faces of his grandchildren gazed back at him with blanching eyes and rigoured grins. When he lifted the two largest heads and parted their matted hair to reveal their features, he was disappointed to find that he still struggled to tell his two daughters apart.

Meanwhile, and from somewhere very far away, his son's voice was announcing how this group of traitors had been halted on the very banks of the Rhine. So shocked had the party of concerned citizens who had found them been that they dispensed immediate justice, as was their inalienable right, with the materials at hand, which happened to be a sharpened ploughshare. All these things Ezekiel heard, but the words and their meaning were mostly lost in the simple, calm realisation that he had already lived far too long. But this wasn't even life any longer, he thought. This was something else.

The scene, the trail, was nearly complete. A kind of silence had fallen across the whole Temple of Reason, and Ezekiel briefly wondered if Roland had finally taken things a little too far. Then, though, he sensed a stirring, and a shift of mood, and looked up. A figure was dragging itself from the corral of accused prisoners, shuffling to ascend the platform where his easel still stood.

Ariadne. Or something like her. She was no longer chained, but it seemed as she raised her hands to remove her hood that her shackles had probably slid off along with the flesh which had liquefied from her bones. The face revealed was far worse than that in the last panel of Ezekiel's triptych. Yet it was the same.

"I am," she said in a quiet voice that scarcely left her tattered lips, yet rang loud in all their heads, "everything that you have heard described. I am the stuff of your dreams and nightmares. I am the scarecrow glimpsed at twilight, and the empty gaze of a charnel-house corpse. If you look at me and do not feel fear, then you are already dead. But let me tell you this—terrible though I am, there is nothing I have done in my long twilight which compares with the deeds I have witnessed this morning. No, you are not monsters. You may think you are, but you aren't. The monster is the idea, the theory, the belief, that cares more for itself than it does for life.

"When, citizens, did you last laugh simply because you felt like laughing? When did you hug your own children? When did you last look up and smile at the sun, or touch a leaf? If you had done any of these things, you would know that life is far too precious to be wasted on some unattainable goal..."

An incredible thing had started to happen to Ariadne as she spoke. Her presence had strengthened, and the vision of what she was began to change. The drooling rents in her cheeks melded. Her scorched and blackened flesh began to re-form. She raised her body, straightened her shoulders. Her ghastly eyes cleared to their full, glorious dark. Even the impression of hair, although grey at first, began to reform. Moment by moment, miracle by miracle, Ariadne was recovering the years which this daylight had taken from her.

Through all of this, Roland had remained silent. Now, though, he stepped forward.

"This creature—" he began.

"No!" Ariadne's voice was powerful now. "Not me, Roland. But *you*. You and all your ilk." She glanced at the judges, the delegates, the guards. All of whom flinched from her glare. "Do you really think that the truth has been found in these creatures, citizens? Are you really now in control of your lives? Or is it not still the lawyers, the book-keepers, the bankers, and the sort of merchants who sell shoddy merchandise then vanish before you can complain? That, and such men as this..." As she gestured towards Roland, Ezekiel saw that even the fingers of her left hand were now whole. "Who talk in bars in the loudest voices and never pay their way and barge to the front of queues and pour their scorn across everything but their own immense self-regard. Not the nobles. No. And not the clergy—at least, not the kind who might baptise your children or come to your sickbed, although there were plenty who would not. But the men who gave the nobles advice, and whispered in their ears, and bowed and smiled and left long rooms walking backwards and talked behind their hands of the debts and bankruptcies of others, and were despicable to their servants and cursed children for playing outside their windows in the street. These are the men we are expected to down to. These are the new, small gods who suck the lifeblood of decency from this country."

Now, as Ariadne spoke, voices were being raised in acclamation and acknowledgment.

"Leave this place, all of you. And let these poor prisoners go. A storm is raging across France, and there is little any of us can do to stop it, but at least we can put an end to this day of killing. Leave now. All of you! Go back to your lives..."

People were murmuring, turning, exchanging embarrassed glances, as if they suddenly found themselves as naked as those sketches. Even some of the judges began to rise from their seats. Then, Roland stepped forward. Once again, he raised his voice and beat his staff, but he did so this time with even greater conviction.

"Citizens!" Much as a dog might when it hears its name, they all stopped and looked towards him. "Have you forgotten who you are and what you hold sacred, and all for the sake of a few words from this lying monstrosity?" He raised his staff, then gestured to the guards. "Kill it! Kill it now—or you will pay with your own lives!"

After all this questioning and uncertainty, Ezekiel saw this order's appeal etched on the men's simple faces. The nearest of the guards, grinning now, or at least grimacing, stepped forward. As he lunged towards Ariadne with the point of his pike, she moved too quickly to be seen, grabbled the shaft and twisted it up. The man found his arms being twisted as well. There was a tearing crack as one and then the other broke. By the time he was starting to fall, still grinning or grimacing and not fully realising what had happened, his nearest colleague somehow had a cutlass jutting from his throat.

Another guard, as he flopped forward and attempted to hold in the slippery spill of his belly, gave an astonished groan.

"I told you all to leave," Ariadne said as the nearest guards began to back away from her. Others, though, perhaps those more used to the horrors of battle, attempted to block her path. One dropped whimpering in a pool of blood. Another, in a blur of black and metal, seemed to cast aside both his legs and sit down on their stumps. Weapons fell. Bodies were cast aside like bloody puppets. Everywhere, there were screams and cries of alarm. Citizens were clambering over each other now in their hurry to get to the west door and escape the Temple of Reason as the one-sided battle continued, and still Roland was shouting for them to fight, stay, destroy this thing. But now he was ignored.

Finally, with the place empty but for the moaning injured and the reek of new blood, Ariadne strode back up the bright central aisle to where Ezekiel still squatted. Her ticking footsteps left a red, wet trail.

"I'm sorry," she muttered as she stood before him, her eyes like holes punched in a dripping mask. "This wasn't how it was supposed to end." She had lost her cape and her hair was clotted and her naked body was streaked in red. She looked like some terrible priestess, and the aura she gave off was sick and cold, and bloody and dark. The apostle-filled windows blazed down on her. Strong though she seemed, he saw her grimace and waver, and knew that whatever strength she had summoned could not last.

"Jesus Christ! By all that is holy...!"

As ever, Roland's voice, had the ring of conviction as he forced open the gilded gate in the rood screen with his staff and tumbled back toward the high alter beyond. With only a flicker of hesitation, Ariadne followed. Slow, but somehow knowing that his own destiny lay here, Ezekiel followed. This was a space that the citizens, either through sloth or atavistic fear, had left almost undisturbed. It was here, away from the eyes of the congregation, that the priests had once raised their wine-filled chalices to the glittering mosaic dome and called upon God to make his presence known, and it seemed to Ezekiel that, on this day of all days, some of that sacred magic still lingered like the echo of lost prayers.

"By all that is sacred..."

Roland was still staggering back. As he did so, he made a clumsy sign of the cross with his dragging staff. This scene would be laughable if it hadn't been so horrible, Ezekiel thought, although he recalled Roland had been a willing enough altar boy back when he was a youth. Now his son was clambering backwards up the very steps of the high alter, and then he was standing on the alter itself, gazed down upon as he raised his staff by a calm-eyed Jesus, a sorrowing Mary, and a stern-looking God.

"Get away from me!"

But still Ariadne walked on. Was she angry? Was it vengeance she sought? Did she feel such emotions at all? What she really seemed, Ezekiel thought, as the long aisles of the choir seemed to extend before him like some great corridor even as he yelled for her to stop, was tired. Now, she was standing before Roland.

"Get back to Hell where you belong!" he cried, before he raised his staff and leapt upon her, driving it hard though her chest.

Ariadne staggered. A fresh stream of darker-seeming blood jetted from her mouth, splattering across gold, gemstones and richly engraved wood. But then she took a step forward, pushing Roland back against the altar and driving the staff even deeper through her body. Even as he screamed and struggled, she took him into her arms and her head and jaws swept back and forth, rending and tearing until she fell forwards and all sounds creased but the patter of blood.

"Ariadne?"

The great distance which had separated Ezekiel from this scene collapsed. He tumbled up the altar steps, drew her back and out from the staff's horrid spike and laid her down on the white marble as his son's head, now hanging from the edge of the alter by little more than a few threads of gristle, looked on.

"Can you hear me?"

He pushed back her hair, thumbed the blood from her lips. Ariadne felt impossibly light. Impossibly cold. Then, in a small shudder, a flicker of the eyelids that briefly revealed something other than dark, she was gone. Ezekiel raised his head and howled in this empty house of a murdered God. Then, quickly, for he knew there was no time to waste, he put his lips to the gore between her breasts and began to drink. He had no idea how long this process lasted, but when he looked up, he saw that the apostles in their windows were already fading, and that all he held in his arms were a few scraps of leathered skin clinging to some ancient bones. Even the thing of deathly horror which he'd described in the final part of his triptych was now gone. With a final glance at the softly glowing windows, the thing that was no longer Ezekiel Morel scurried off in search of some darker place to await the fall of night.